CLASSIC COLLECTION

ROBINSON CRUSOE

DANIEL DEFOE

ADAPTED BY SAVIOUR PIROTTA · ILLUSTRATED BY ALESSANDRO BALDANZI

SWEET WATER PRESS

Disaster at Sea

I was born in 1632, in the English city of York. My father was very keen for me to become a lawyer, but I was far more interested in going to sea. As soon as I was old enough, I boarded a ship bound for distant lands.

For a while, my seafaring brought me luck and fortune. I bought goods in one port and sold them in another, making a huge profit. I even managed to buy a coffee plantation in Brazil. Then one day I was sailing along the coast of South America, when our ship was caught in a storm.

The wind blew us off course so when the captain saw land through his telescope he did not know where we were. Hoping to find shelter, he steered the ship toward the land. Alas, we hit sand in shallow water long before we reached the shore. In no time at all the ship was flooded and sinking. We hastily lowered a small boat into the heaving waves.

However, the sea was so rough that the boat was soon overturned. We were flung into the sea and I began swimming. I don't know how long I struggled in the sea, but I do remember it was starting to get dark when I felt sharp pebbles under my feet.

By some miracle, I made it to shore alive. Coughing up water, I dragged myself out of the sea and crawled up onto gritty sand.

Alone and Lost

I searched the deserted beach but there was no sign of my companions from the ship. Then a horrible thought struck me: What if there were dangerous creatures that would pounce on me and tear me limb from limb? I had to find somewhere safe to spend the night. I hurried up the beach to a tropical jungle. There I climbed into a tree and, settling down on a huge branch, fell into a deep sleep.

When I woke up, the sun was shining. The wind had dropped and the sea was calm. To my amazement, I could see our wrecked ship. The wind and tide had brought it closer to shore and she was trapped on a sandbar.

I called out, hoping one of my companions would answer back. No one did. I was alone. Alone and lost! I had no idea if I was back on the coast of South America or stranded on a small island. No one had come to take a closer look at the wreck. That meant the place must be uninhabited. I didn't have a single soul to share my troubles with.

For a while I sat on a rock, feeling sorry for myself. Then I said to myself, "Cheer up. Do you not realize how lucky you are? Your shipmates are all dead but you are still alive. If you are to survive until a ship passes by, you are going to need all your skills."

Back on Board

My first task was to find fresh water. Nothing had passed my lips for hours and I was parched. I set off into the jungle, which was quite hilly and filled with flowers of every shape and color. Once I found a spring of fresh water, I had a long drink and washed my face and hands. Nearby the birds were feasting on strange fruit the size of my fist.

I plucked one and, squashing it open with my fingers, ate the ripe flesh. I didn't know what the fruit was called but it was delicious. Picking some more, I stuffed them into my pockets for later and returned to the shore.

By now the tide was low, and the wrecked ship looked so close I knew I could swim to it. I waded out as far as I could, then swam toward it.

The next time I looked up, the hull was towering above me. I could see a rope dangling over the side, its end knot just within reach. Grabbing it with both hands, I hauled myself up. A loud bark greeted 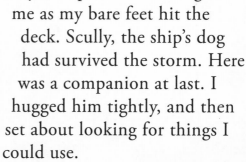 me as my bare feet hit the deck. Scully, the ship's dog had survived the storm. Here was a companion at last. I hugged him tightly, and then set about looking for things I could use.

In the food chest, I found bread and cheese, and dried goat's meat cut into strips. There was a bag of wheat too, which the cook had meant to grind into flour. I also found the cook's knife, stuck in a big wheel of cheese.

From the storeroom, I dragged out a carpenter's chest full of tools. I also took a couple of swords, some muskets, a bag of shot, and a cask of gunpowder. They would all come in handy if I needed to go hunting.

In the captain's cabin I found a bag of silver coins and a Bible. I took the holy book and also the coins with me, even though I couldn't imagine what use money would be on an uninhabited island.

Once I had piled all the things on deck, I had to find a way to get them safely to shore. There were lots of wooden planks floating around the ship. I lashed them together with rope and made a raft.

Then I carefully lowered my goods onto it. When the tide came in, I climbed down, taking the dog with me, and hoped the current would carry me to land.

As I sat down on the carpenter's chest, I felt a thump behind me. The dog barked, and I turned to see that the ship's cat had joined us.

My little family was growing.

My Island Home

After a quick lunch, I climbed to the top of the hill to get my bearings. My new home was a small island. There were no houses, no sign of habitation, just dense jungle. I could see land far away across the sea, but I could not tell whether it was the coast of South America or just a bigger island.

During the climb, I also found the perfect spot to pitch my camp. It was a flat piece of land, halfway up a hill overlooking the beach I had landed on. From there I could see out over the ocean, but anyone approaching the island would not see me unless I wanted them to. My little piece of land, my new home, was well screened with bushes. Clean water trickled in a stream nearby.

I hurried back down to the shore and, one by one, fetched the goods I had salvaged. I arranged them all around me in a circle, the dog sitting

on the carpenter's chest, the cat licking her paws on the cask of gunpowder. It was dark now, and I was tired. I read the Bible for a while, thanking God for all the provisions he had sent me, and for rescuing me from the storm.

And then I slept.

During the next few days, I ventured out to the wrecked ship no less than twelve times. I managed to bring back some heavy canvas and bits of sail that had been ripped off by the storm.

I also found more tools and ammunition for my guns, wooden buckets, the cook's grindstone, some fishing hooks and line, and a battered telescope. Going back to my old quarters to retrieve my hammock, I found another cat lying in it. I scooped it up and carried it to the raft.

The poor creature was lucky I found her that day. The same night, a sudden storm blew up and smashed our ship to pieces.

The next day I used the canvas to make a proper tent, in which I strung up my hammock. But I still didn't feel secure against any wild beast that might come charging over the hills.

So I set about building a wooden wall, a palisade, around my tent. I did this by hacking trees into stakes and driving them into the ground. Soon I had my own little fortress to protect me. There was no door or gate. I made a wooden ladder, which I lifted after me every time I went in or out of my new home.

I also hollowed out a little cave in the hill behind me. I put all the gunpowder I had rescued from the ship in the cave, so it would not get damp in the rain.

I realized that I would soon lose track of time unless I kept a record. On the exact spot where I had crawled out of the water, I hammered a wooden post in the ground. This became my calendar. Every day, I carved a notch in it with my knife.

Time passes quickly when you have so many things to do. I built myself a chair and table. My old clothes were becoming ragged, so I sewed new ones from the bits of ragged sail. I caught wild hares to eat, and made clothes from fur. I even made myself a large umbrella to keep the hot sun off my face.

I grew wheat from the grain I had found in the cook's store and made flour from it. That first mouthful of bread, baked in a clay oven I made, tasted better than anything I had ever eaten.

One day I found a goat caught in one of my rabbit traps. It was bleating so sadly, I released her. She followed me home, with her kids trotting after her. From that day I never lacked for fresh milk and even learned to make cheese.

I trapped a parrot which I named Poll. He loved snatching food out of my hand, but, try as I might, I could not get him to say a word.

And so the notches on the wooden post increased, until five years had passed and my skin had turned a deep, nutty brown.

The Canoe

One day I had an idea to build a canoe. It might carry me across the sea to the distant land I could see from the top of the hill.

I felled a large cedar tree with my ax and started hollowing it out. It was backbreaking work. Chopping the tree down took a month, hollowing it out another three months. But at last I finished it. Now all I had to do was drag it down to the water. This is when I realized I'd made a big mistake.

The canoe was too far from the beach, and too heavy to drag across stony ground. I thought about digging a channel from the shore to it but I calculated it would take at least twelve years to finish. So I abandoned the canoe, and with it all hope of leaving the island. As I cooked my dinner that night, I felt lonelier than I ever had in my entire life. But as I sat down to my meal, a shrill voice made me jump.

"Poor Robinson Crusoe. Poor Robinson Crusoe. Where are you, Robinson Crusoe?"

It was Poll the parrot. He had spoken at last, but they were not words I had tried to teach him. Then I remembered that I talked to myself like that when I was feeling sad about being stuck on the island. Poll had copied me, and the sound of his voice was a greater comfort to me than anyone could imagine.

Visitors

A year or so after I had abandoned my canoe, I started building a much smaller sailing boat. It gave me great pleasure to sail around my little island, discovering new coves and beaches. But it would never take me across the sea.

One day I was walking to my boat when I saw a footprint in the sand. For a moment I thought it was my own. Then I realized that the foot that had made it was much smaller than mine.

There was someone else on the island, someone who had arrived unnoticed. I shivered in my furry clothes. Who could this stranger be? Where on the island was he hiding? And was he friendly, or a man-eating cannibal?

I hurried home to fetch my telescope. Then, making sure the dog or the goats were not following, I set out to explore every inch of the island. If I had a visitor, I wanted to know where he was.

That afternoon, I ventured much farther from my little fortress than I had ever done before. In some parts of the island the hills were very steep and I'd had no reason to climb them before. That day, reaching the top of one, I put the telescope to my eye and looked out to sea. There was a boat bobbing on the waves, a canoe with perhaps six or eight people—I couldn't tell exactly how many from this far away. They were paddling away from my island, their backs to me.

I watched until the boat disappeared into the distance. Now I could smell smoke wafting up from the beach below. I hurried down, toward the remains of a bonfire I could see in the sand. When I came close to it, I stopped and stared in horror. The ashes from the fire were still smoldering, and scattered all around were skulls and the remains of other human bones.

The sight of those charred bones chilled me to the core. I had heard about cannibals before. I knew they were dangerous, and I was determined not to be captured by them.

Returning home, I decided to start burning charcoal instead of wood on my cooking fire. It would make less smoke that could be seen by the cannibals. Looking for wood to make charcoal, I stumbled across the mouth of a tunnel, hidden behind some bushes at the foot of a hill.

I managed to wriggle inside and discovered it led to the most amazing underground cave. The walls and roof were covered in stalactites, which glittered like multicolored jewels in the light of a candle I had brought with me.

Here was a safe hiding place for my guns and powder. It would make perfect sleeping quarters too if the cannibals ever returned. Once inside the tunnel, I could easily block up the entrance with a rock.

A Daring Rescue

Luckily many years passed and the cannibals did not return. Scully the dog and the cats grew old and died. Poll the parrot passed away too, and I caught and tamed some more birds, which, together with my growing herd of goats, kept me company. If I had not been worried that the cannibals might return, I believe I would have been quite happy to stay on that little paradise for the rest of my life.

Then one day I saw a wisp of smoke rising above the trees some two miles up the coast. My heart skipped a beat. Was it the cannibals again?

I fetched my telescope and a musket, and keeping to the shadow of the trees, crept along the coast. I stopped above a creek where I had often come to fish. On the other side of it, I could see no less than thirty men dancing around a fire. They had two canoes pulled up on the sand. Tied to a tree nearby were two other men.

Three of the dancing men approached the tree and, whooping loudly, slashed the ropes holding the prisoners. One was immediately hit on the head with a club. The other, finding himself free for a moment, screamed and sprinted toward the creek.

Three of the cannibals around the fire grabbed their bows and arrows and ran after him. They came to the water and two dived into the creek after the fugitive, their bows slung over their shoulders.

Quickly, I slid from my hiding place and, after waiting for the escaped prisoner to clamber out of the water, rushed at the men chasing him. I hit the first one with the end of the telescope and sent him reeling back into the creek. The second one, though, saw me and leaped sideways onto the beach.

His hand reached out to the bow on his shoulder. I knew he meant to shoot me, so I whipped out my musket and fired at him.

The blast from my gun made the fugitive rigid with shock. His eyes grew wide and he stared in horror at my musket. I patted him on the shoulder and smiled to show that I was a friend.

"We'd better go if you don't want to be captured again," I said out loud.

And then I turned and ran back into the trees. The man followed me, mostly because the cannibals on the beach were starting to run toward us.

Before long we reached the safety of my hideout, and the man fell to his knees in front of me. He placed my foot on his head to show me that I was now his master.

"Now, now," I said, pulling him to his feet. "I need a friend, not a slave. My name is Robinson Crusoe. What is yours?"

The man did not seem to understand. "Today is Friday," I said. "Your lucky day. I think I shall call you Friday."

Friday

The next day, Friday and I returned to the creek to see if the cannibals had left. There was no sign of them, or their canoes. The traces of their fire were still visible though, and the beach was littered with bones.

"Is it not horrific?" I said to Friday. But he did not seem at all upset at the sight of the human remains. I suspected he too had eaten human flesh in the past.

I was determined to educate my new friend, so I roasted a goat over the fire and gave him the meat to eat on some bread. His eyes shone at the taste of it.

"Goat, good," I said.

"Goat, good," he repeated.

I pinched the flesh on my arm.

"Man-flesh, not good."

"Man-flesh, not good," echoed Friday.

Still, I knew I'd be foolish to trust the fellow just yet. I made him a tent to sleep in outside the palisade.

So began one of the happiest times of my life. I set about teaching Friday to speak English. I taught him how to grow crops and tame birds. I also spoke to him about my belief in God.

Soon I realized I did not need to worry about Friday harming me. He was loyal and trustworthy, and the best friend I'd ever had. Once he'd learned enough English to hold a proper conversation, we often talked long into the night.